The Bippolo Seed
and Other Lost Stories
by Dr. Seuss

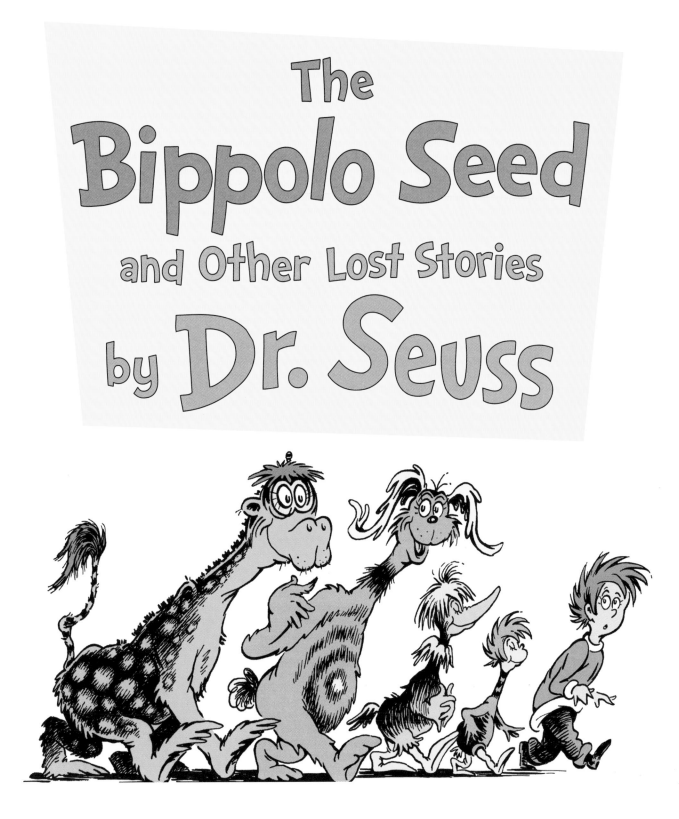

Introduction by **CHARLES D. COHEN**

RANDOM HOUSE 🏠 NEW YORK

TM & copyright © by Dr. Seuss Enterprises, L.P. 2011
Introduction copyright © 2011 by Charles D. Cohen

All rights reserved. Published in the United States by Random House Children's Books, a division of Random House, Inc., New York. The stories and illustrations in this collection were originally published separately in slightly different form in *Redbook* magazine: "The Bippolo Seed" (June 1951), "The Rabbit, the Bear, and the Zinniga-Zanniga" (February 1951), "Gustav the Goldfish" (June 1950), "Tadd and Todd" (August 1950), "Steak for Supper" (November 1950), "The Strange Shirt Spot" (September 1951), and "The Great Henry McBride" (November 1951).

Random House and the colophon are registered trademarks of Random House, Inc.

Visit us on the Web!
www.randomhouse.com/kids
Seussville.com

Educators and librarians, for a variety of teaching tools, visit us at www.randomhouse.com/teachers

Library of Congress Cataloging-in-Publication Data
Seuss, Dr.
The Bippolo Seed and other lost stories / by Dr. Seuss ;
with introduction by Charles D. Cohen. — 1st ed.
   p. cm.
Summary: Presents seven Dr. Seuss stories first published in magazines between 1948 and 1959, with an introduction.
Contents: The Bippolo Seed — The rabbit, the bear, and the Zinniga-Zanniga — Gustav the Goldfish — Tadd and Todd — Steak for supper — The strange shirt spot — The great Henry McBride.
ISBN 978-0-375-86435-3 (trade) — ISBN 978-0-375-96435-0 (lib. bdg.)
1. Children's stories, American. [1. Stories in rhyme. 2. Short stories.]
I. Cohen, Charles D. II. Title.
PZ8.3.G276Bhp 2010 [E]—dc22 2009052588

Printed in the United States of America   10 9   First Edition

Random House Children's Books supports the First Amendment and celebrates the right to read.

Contents

Introduction

CHARLES D. COHEN is the world's foremost Seuss scholar and collector of Seussiana. Dr. Cohen is the author of The Seuss, the Whole Seuss, and Nothing but the Seuss, *the definitive visual biography of Theodor Seuss Geisel. He is a graduate of Haverford College and the Tufts University School of Dental Medicine.*

Buried treasure! People, young and old, love the idea of it. Stories, books, and movies have led us to believe that with luck, persistence, and cleverness, we just might find something valuable that no one else knows about. The fact that geological excavations and underwater recovery expeditions have unearthed dinosaur skeletons, ancient artwork, and sunken ships only fans the flames of imaginations already fueled by a host of urban legends. This desire for discovery creates a curious communal yearning in the wake of a beloved artist's death. The hope arises that somewhere—in a desk drawer, an attic, or a publisher's vault—some unpublished manuscript lies waiting to be discovered. Our appetite whetted, we hunger for someone to unearth one last great work.

In the case of Ted Geisel—best known as Dr. Seuss— I am happy to say that our fondest dreams have come true! A number of lost stories were hiding in places that could be found without a treasure map. From 1948 through 1959, Ted Geisel published a series of short works that appeared in magazines, most of which were tossed out when the next month's issue arrived. Over time, these stories were largely forgotten. But after tracing references to them, I traveled to libraries to research their collections of these old magazines; investigated, photocopied, and chronicled the stories; and eventually tracked down and purchased copies of the original magazines through the Internet. The discovery was thrilling—I was reading Dr. Seuss stories that few people even knew existed!

These stories each highlight an aspect of what made Dr. Seuss who he was. The first and last stories are great examples of Ted's "message" stories, with "The Bippolo Seed" providing a strong antigreed moral and "The Great Henry McBride" trumpeting the importance of the imagination. "The Rabbit, the Bear, and the Zinniga-Zanniga" and "Tadd and Todd" demonstrate Ted's craftsmanship and mastery of rhythm and rhyme. "Steak for Supper" adds a host of marvelous beasts to his menagerie. Finally, "Gustav, the Goldfish" and "The Strange Shirt Spot" are adventure stories, in which a child left to his own devices solves a fantastic problem. These stories are great examples of what made Dr. Seuss such a giant in the world of children's books.

"The Bippolo Seed" is the tale of a duck with a practical wish for a week's worth of food, who winds up asking for things he can't possibly use. In the process, a story about good luck becomes a warning about greed.

Four months before he died, Ted was contacted by a woman

who, as a child, had fallen in love with "The Bippolo Seed" and was now hoping to see it published in book form. In spite of his failing health, Ted took the time to write to her on May 20, 1991, just before the fortieth anniversary of the story's publication. He thanked her "for still liking that old story" and explained, "For some reason or other it never found its way into a book. But, since you still like it, maybe now it will!" Twenty years later, his hopeful prediction has finally come true, and "The Bippolo Seed" is the first story in this collection.

"The Rabbit, the Bear, and the Zinniga-Zanniga," a story about a rabbit who saves himself from a bear via a single eyelash, features the quirky humor that children love in Dr. Seuss stories. It also has the flawless pacing, meter, rhyme, and patented Seussian moral, distilled into a final rhyming couplet, that readers have come to expect in a book by Dr. Seuss.

This David and Goliath theme occurs often in his work. In "Yertle the Turtle," it is Mack, the lowly bottom turtle on the stack, who burps and topples King Yertle from his imperious perch. Mighty King Derwin would have destroyed the Kingdom of Didd were it not for the cleverness of a menial page boy in *Bartholomew and the Oobleck*. And Jo-Jo, who is small even by the standards of the tiny Whos, saves their dust-speck world from annihilation in *Horton Hears a Who!*

Early editions of the popular Beginner Book *A Fish out of Water* included a claim on the dust jacket that the author, Helen Palmer, was "married to an eccentric writer, Theo. LeSieg (himself a Beginner Book author)." By now, many people know that "LeSieg" is "Geisel" spelled backward and that Helen

Palmer was Ted Geisel's first wife. What few people know is that her book was based on one of Ted's lost stories, "Gustav, the Goldfish."

The basic stories in "Gustav" and *A Fish out of Water* are identical—a goldfish gets fed too much and grows progressively larger, being transferred from fishbowl to flower bowl to kitchen pots to bathtub and finally ending up in the cellar. The main differences are that Helen's version does not rhyme and the illustrations are by Phil (P. D.) Eastman (with whom Ted worked in the army and who created the wildly successful Beginner Book *Go, Dog. Go!*).

Redbook originally published "Gustav, the Goldfish" in June 1950, and it has been floundering in obscurity ever since. Now, for the first time in over sixty years, you can see the original Dr. Seuss version of the story, with his characteristic rhythm and rhyme and matchless illustrations.

Twins are one of the most frequently recurring images in Ted Geisel's work. His fascination with them began in childhood, and he continued to encounter multiple births in a variety of forms throughout his life. When he was eight years old, conjoined twins Mary and Margaret Gibb were born in Holyoke, Massachusetts, just north of Ted's Springfield home. They probably contributed to Ted's fanciful imaginings, and he often chose to join his twins together—frequently by their beards.

Childhood is fraught with many difficulties, and twins face the additional challenge of balancing their own individuality against a shared identity with their sibling. Ted recognized this problem of twindom, and his sympathy for their plight struck a chord with generations of twins who received "Tadd and Todd" in faded black-and-white photocopies over the decades. Ted's twins finally make their vibrant reappearance here, in one of the best of Dr. Seuss's lost stories.

One of the greatest pleasures of almost any Dr. Seuss story is the wonderfully bizarre bestiary that populates it, and "Steak for Supper" has crazy characters to spare. In November 1950, when "Steak" was first published in *Redbook,* it introduced five new species of wildlife—the Ikka, the Gritch, the Grickle, the Nupper, and a pair of Wild Wheef. Ted began experimenting with odd beasts at least as early as age nineteen. In the November 26, 1923, issue of Dartmouth's student magazine, Ted invented creatures from the island of Bo-Bo, like the Dingle-bläder, the Heumkia, and the Blvgk. From that starting point, Ted's menagerie of imaginary animals continued to grow. The preposterous posse in "Steak for Supper" reminds us of the joy and thrill of strange new things we may encounter when we read a Dr. Seuss story for the first time.

If something about "The Strange Shirt Spot" seems familiar, it's probably not because you read it in the September 1951 issue of *Redbook.* Ted Geisel expanded the idea behind "The Strange Shirt Spot" into the bathtub-ring scene in *The Cat in the Hat Comes Back.*

In both the story and the later book, the strange spot is transferred from one object to another before the idea arises to try to put it outside the house. Ted felt strongly that although his stories could start with one outrageous element, everything thereafter had to follow logically. Because the original story had to be shorter, Ted confined the action within the house, so a broom was used to sweep up the stubborn spot. In the book, Ted allowed the stain to spread outside, where a more elaborate weapon was needed to battle it—thus "broom" became the explosive "Voom." Only Ted Geisel could expand a simple stain to create such a scene, one of the most memorable in any Dr. Seuss book.

Daydreaming is a theme that comes up in several Dr. Seuss stories, beginning with *And to Think That I Saw It on Mulberry Street,* the first of Ted's books to be published. In that story, young Marco has a dull walk to school every day, which he enlivens by imagining a fabulous parade along the route he travels.

Marco returned ten years later in *McElligot's Pool,* still daydreaming, this time about a menagerie of fish. In *If I Ran the Zoo,* it was Gerald McGrew who did the daydreaming, imagining what a zoo would look like if he were in charge. In these stories, no matter which kid is creating the fantasies, most of the grown-ups just don't get it.

In "The Great Henry McBride," young Henry fantasizes about the many exciting careers he could pursue, without the limitations an adult might anticipate. Ted loved the idea of a kid who could dream without restraint. A child at heart, he never felt limited in his choice of careers either. Originally planning to be a teacher, he went into cartooning instead, branched out into advertising, began illustrating books for other people, painted murals in homes and clubs, started a weekly comic strip, created sculptures to sell by mail order, planned to be a novelist but then tried writing for children instead, and wound up becoming one of the bestselling children's book authors of all time.

But even all of *those* jobs weren't enough for him! After his first four children's books came out, he switched to drawing political cartoons full-time, joined the army, discovered animation and learned about filmmaking, then moved to Hollywood to try to make his living as a screenwriter. Ted finished the first draft of a screenplay for the feature film *The 5000 Fingers of Dr. T* just four months before "The Great Henry McBride" was published in the November 1951 issue of *Redbook*. He was literally writing this story while he was trying to establish himself in yet *another* profession.

Unlike the disapproving adults in many of his stories, Ted didn't believe that Henry was silly or confused in musing about multiple careers. After all, Ted found success in a variety of occupations. Well beyond childhood, Ted Geisel continued to dream and succeed without limits. He truly *was* the real-life Great Henry McBride!

Although most of the original magazines were discarded half a century ago, these lost stories made an impression on people who were fortunate enough to have read them. One blogger fondly recalled that her favorite story was "The Bippolo Seed," which, as a child, she memorized and performed with puppets. At a Dr. Seuss museum exhibition I curated, another person excitedly explained to me that she and her sister had been given a faded photocopy of "Tadd and Todd," a story that was handed down from one generation of twins to another. While I was working on this collection, I received an email from a woman whose mother used to read her "The Rabbit, the Bear, and the Zinniga-Zanniga" and then, when the magazine pages had worn to shreds, typed the story up for her. She contacted me because she had searched the Internet but couldn't "find any indication of its existence." Fortunately for these die-hard fans—and the rest of us—these wonderful stories have not been lost. This collection includes all of the original text and artwork that first appeared more than fifty years ago—with a color palette that is enhanced well beyond the limitations of the magazines of that time.

These stories reflect a change in Ted's approach to writing for children. Before World War II, he did not consider his children's books particularly important. But after observing German and Japanese children reared on propaganda (which he called "the worst educational crime in the entire history of the world"), he began to take his work more seriously, developing a new philosophy about educating children through reading.

In addition to this new mission, something else changed in Ted's writing several years after his army service. By January 1950, ten Dr. Seuss stories had been published, only four of which rhymed. But a chance encounter the previous summer wound up being a revelation for Ted. After he gave a lecture at a writing conference in Salt Lake City, a local family offered to show Ted the city's famous lake. Excited to be with Dr. Seuss, their son Brad—who was reportedly less than three years old—recited by heart Ted's most recent book, *Thidwick the Big-Hearted Moose.* Ted marveled, "I don't write for kids that young. . . . How does he do it?"

The fact was that the boy couldn't read *Thidwick,* but he had been able to memorize *how the words sounded.* Nearly eight years later, in the November 17, 1957, edition of the *New York Times Book Review,* Ted called upon that experience to criticize the way people wrote for young children:

School book publishing houses all have . . . lists . . . of words that kids can be expected to read, at various stages in their progress through the elementary grades. How they compile these lists is still a mystery to me. But somehow or other . . . with divining rods or something . . . they've figured out the number of words that a teacher can ram into the average child's noodle. (Also the approximate dates on which these rammings should take place.)

Poor Orlo! At the age of 6½, his noodle has scarcely been rammed at all!

He can, of course, recognize some 1,500 *spoken* words when they enter his head through the holes in his ears. But . . . he can recognize only about 300 when they try to get into his head through his eyes. All the other printed words in the world all look, to Orlo, like Appomatox [*sic*].

For Ted, books and stories had always been primarily visual experiences. Coming from a background in cartooning and advertising, he was concerned with creating eye-catching illustrations and with the way the written word appeared on the page. After his visit to Utah, Ted had a new appreciation for the way his words *sounded.* He began to experiment with stories that appeared in *Redbook* and *Children's Activities,* tales with lively auditory appeal that he intended to be read aloud to children by their parents. Ted introduced the first of the stories by saying that it was "presented to you with a technique that's new."

The first of these newly styled stories was published in June 1950, which proved to be a pivotal point in Dr. Seuss's writing career. It was so important to Ted to use the sound of his words to get kids to want to learn to read that he couldn't wait for just one or two books to be published a year. In the eighteen months after the first of these experimental stories appeared, there was only one Dr. Seuss book for Random House to publish, but fourteen read-aloud Dr. Seuss stories appeared in *Redbook* and a fifteenth one was released only as a phonograph record, which *had* to be heard rather than read.

He concentrated so much on these efforts that, as he explained in the May 11, 1958, *New York Times Book Review,* while he didn't "expect to revolutionize teaching methods," he did "hope to make learning new words more fun than it is at present." His new approach was so successful that he ended up doing both.

These rediscovered treasures from the departed master allow the world to relish anew his beloved and unique style. But they also enable us to view writing and artwork from a transitional period that was critical to the development of the Dr. Seuss we know today. I hope that you will find these tales as fascinating and endearing as I do. For me, they are like finding a silver box containing a Bippolo Seed. . . .

The Bippolo Seed

One bright sunny day, a young duck named McKluck
Had a wonderful, wonderful piece of good luck.
He was walking along when he spied on the ground
A marvelous thing that is quite seldom found.
'Twas a small silver box. And it looked mighty old
And on top of the box, it was written in gold:
"Who finds this rare box will be lucky, indeed,
For inside this box is a Bippolo Seed!
Plant it and wish! And then count up to three!
Whatever you wish for, whatever it be
Will sprout and grow out of a Bippolo Tree!"
"Well!" thought the duck. "Well, now, what do you know!
I just have to wish, and my wishes will grow.
Now, what'll I wish for . . . ? Now, what do I need . . . ?
Don't need very much . . . only food for my feed.
So I wish," said the duck as he opened his beak,
"I wish for some duck food. Enough for a week."

Then he dug a quick hole. But before he could drop
The seed in the ground, a loud voice shouted, *"Stop!"*
The duck looked around and he saw a big cat.
"Now *why,*" asked the cat, "did you wish for just that?
One week's worth of duck food! Pooh! That's not enough.
Why, *I'd* wish for five hundred pounds of the stuff!"
"But, gosh," said the duck with the Bippolo Seed,
"Five hundred pounds is much more than I need."
"But that's just the point," said the cat. "For you see,
When you grow all that food on your Bippolo Tree,
You can go into business . . . in business with me!
We'll *sell* all that food. You'll be rich!" laughed the kitty.
"Why, you'll be the richest young duck in this city!"
"Hmm . . . ," said the duck, and he wrinkled his brow.
"I never thought much about money till now.

But, golly, you're right.
With some money, gee whiz,
Why, I'd be the happiest
duck that there is!

I'll wish for that food." But the cat called, "*Not yet!*
We'll think of some *more* things to wish for, I'll bet.
Why, *I* know a very nice thing you could wish . . .
A tree that grows duck food could also grow fish!
Wish six hundred fish to grow out of the ground
And we'll sell those fish at a dollar a pound!
Now, a dollar a pound is a very high rate.
Say, you'll be the richest young duck in this state!"
"Why, sure!" smiled the duck. "I most certainly will!"
"But, Duck," said the cat, "you can be richer *still*!
Why wish for a little? Why not for a lot?
The bigger the wish, the more money you've got!"
"That's right!" clucked the duck, and he chuckled with glee.
"I'll wish for some oysters to grow on my tree!
I'll wish for my tree to grow doughnuts and crullers!
I'll wish for my tree to grow skates and umbrellas!"

"Fine," cheered the cat. "Now you're doing just grand.

Say! You'll be the richest young duck in this land!"

"You wait!" bragged the duck. "I'll do better than that.

You listen to this!" he called out to the cat.

"I'll wish for ten bicycles made out of pearls!

And eight hundred muffs that we'll sell to small girls!

I'll wish for some eyeglasses! Nine hundred pair!

And one thousand shirts made of kangaroo hair!

A ton of stuffed olives, with cherries inside!

And ten tons of footballs, with crocodile hide!

We'll sell them for cash in our wonderful store

In the Notions Department. The forty-ninth floor."

Then he took a deep breath, and he wished for still more. . . .

"I wish," yelled the duck, and he started to scream,

"For eight thousand buckets of purple ice cream!

A trunk full of toothpaste! A big kitchen sink!

And lots of brass keyholes! And gallons of ink!

I wish for two boatloads of Baked Boston Beans!

And, also, nine carloads of sewing machines!"

Then his mouth started steaming, his tongue got so hot.

But the more that he wished, the more greedy he got.

"I wish," shrieked the duck, "for a million silk towels!

And three million cages for very big owls!

And forty-five thousand, two hundred and two

Hamburger buns! And a bottle of glue!

And four million satin-lined red rubber boots!

And five million banjos! And six million flutes!

Oranges! Apples! And all kinds of fruits!

And nine billion Hopalong Cassidy suits!

Yes, *that's* what I wish for, by Jimminy Gee!
And when they sprout out on my Bippolo Tree,
Say, I'll be the richest young duck in this world!"
And he got so excited, he whirled and he twirled!
And that duck got so dizzy and crazy with greed
That he waved both his arms, and the Bippolo Seed
Slipped out of his fist and flew high in the sky
And it landed *"Kerplunk!"* in a river nearby!
Then it sank in the river and drifted away.
And that cat and that duck, all the rest of that day,
Dived deep in that river, but never did see
A trace of the Seed of the Bippolo Tree.
And the chances are good that this greedy pair never
Will find such a wonderful seed again, ever.
But *if* they should find one, that cat and that duck
Won't wish for so much. And they'll have better luck.

The Rabbit, the Bear,
and the Zinniga-Zanniga

Once of upon of a time, way down south,

Lived a very big bear with a very big mouth

And very big teeth in his very big jaws

And very big claws in his very big paws.

And this very big bear, who was hunting for meat,

One day spied a rabbit who looked good to eat.

"A-ha!" thought the bear. "He looks tender, all right!

Oh, boy! I'll have rabbit for supper tonight!"

So, on his big feet, he crept up to the rabbit.

He crouched very low and leaned forward to grab it,

But, just as his jaws were 'bout ready to nab it,

The rabbit looked up and he saw the bear's face.

"Oh-oh!" gulped the rabbit. "I'm in a bad place!

I cannot escape. And I see with a glance

That it's no use to fight, 'cause I haven't a chance

For I am a rabbit with very small jaws
And very small claws in my very small paws.
Alas!" thought the rabbit. "This moment's my last
Unless I *think* terribly, terribly fast. . . .
I've got to be smart! Got to think of some trick!"
And that little old rabbit, he thought mighty quick!
Then, just as the teeth of the bear touched his head,
The rabbit jumped up and he suddenly said,
"One, two, three, four, five, six . . . seven . . . eight . . . nine!
Nine . . . ? Only *nine* . . . ? That's a very bad sign!
Poor bear!" sighed the rabbit, then counted again.
And this time, he counted from one up to *ten*!
"Huh . . . ?" the bear grunted. He stared and he stopped.
He looked mighty puzzled. His jaw sort of dropped.
"Now, what were you counting, then? What did you see?
Do you mean to say something's the matter with me?"
"Err . . . well," said the rabbit, from down where he stood.
"I sure hate to tell you. It isn't too good.
I was counting the eyelashes 'round your two eyes,
Your left eye . . . your right eye . . . and, to my surprise,
They weren't the same number!
        Almost, but not quite.
You've *ten* on your *left* eye,
        but *nine* on your *right*!
I'm sorry . . . *SO* sorry.
        But, sir, it is true.
Poor bear! This is dreadful!
        One eyelash too few!"

The bear looked upset. He looked frightfully sad.
"Good gracious!" he gasped. "Is *that* really so bad?"
"Err . . . well," said the rabbit. "I've counted the hairs
That grow on the eyelids of hundreds of bears
And I always have noticed, in adding up theirs,
That they always come out to an even amount.
But *yours,* Mr. Bear, make an *un*-even count!
And I guess that's the reason," the rabbit then said,
"For the lop-sided way that you're holding your head.
It's twisted! It's sagging! Because of the weight
Of your un-even lashes, you can't hold it straight!"

"My head . . . ?" groaned the bear with an unhappy roar.
"Why, I never knew it was crooked before!
But, now that you say so, it *does* feel quite funny!"
"I'll bet that it hurts you a lot," said the bunny.
"I'll bet that it hurts you right down to your tail!
My! My! Mr. Bear, you look horribly pale!
Say . . . ! How does your *throat* feel? A little bit prickly?"
"It *does*!" moaned the bear. "And my stomach feels tickly!
Poor me!" cried the bear. "I feel all-over sickly!"
"Tch! Tch!" said the rabbit. "It's just as I reckoned.
Your ailment is getting much worse by the second.
Your tongue, Mr. Bear . . . Does it taste a bit fuzzy?
Your brain, Mr. Bear . . . Does it feel a bit wuzzy?"
"Why, yes!" gasped the bear. "It most certainly does!
Is that a bad sign . . . all that fuzz and that wuzz?"
"It is," said the rabbit. "Alas and alack!
It's a sign that your trouble has spread to your back.
For, even right now, while I'm standing here speaking,
I hear a loud sound from your backbone! It's *creaking*!
Oh, the lack of an eyelash can make you a wreck.
The lack of an eyelash can break a bear's neck!
It can break all your ribs! It can ruin your heart!
Who knows what might happen! You *may* fall apart!
Be careful, poor bear! Don't you even dare cough
Or your feet and your tail and your nose may fall off!"
And he gave that big bear such a sorrowful look
That the bear started trembling. He shook and he shook.
"Ah, me!" the bear blubbered. "Oh, what can I do?
Must I die just because of one eyelash too few?

Oh, *HOW* can I get one more eyelash to grow . . . !"

"Err, well," smiled the rabbit. "It happens I know

Of a way you *might* do it. You're standing, you see,

Right under a Zinniga-Zanniga Tree!

Now, the flowers of this tree have some wonderful juices

That doctors have put to some marvelous uses.

Their juice, I am told, is so strong that it cures

Sicknesses even much greater than yours.

The juice of these flowers cures measles and mumps.

The juice of these flowers cures freckles and bumps.

Whooping cough! Croup! Also colic and sprains!

Chickenpox! Smallpox! And belly-ache pains!

There's *nothing,* they say, that this juice cannot do.

So I think, Mr. Bear, it's the right juice for you.

What *you* ought to do, least it seems so to me,

Is climb up this Zinniga-Zanniga Tree

And pick yourself one of these wonderful flowers.

Hold it tight to your eye for a couple of hours,

And I know it'll cure you. I haven't a doubt!

For the lash you are lacking will suddenly sprout!"

"You mean," cried the bear, "I'll have ten on each eye?

You mean," cried the bear, "that I don't have to die?

Oh, thanks!" cried the bear. "You are wonderfully good."

And he climbed up that tree just as fast as he could.

And, while that big bear held the flower to his face,
The rabbit, like lightning, raced off from that place!
And, thus, he escaped from the very big jaws
Of that very big bear with the very big claws,
And he laughed as he ran on his very small paws:
"It's always the same
    when you fight with Big Guys . . .
A bit of Quick-Thinking
    counts much more than size!"

Gustav, the Goldfish

The man who sold Gustav the Goldfish to us
Had warned us, *"Take care!* When you feed this small cuss
Just feed him a spot. If you feed him a lot,
Then something might happen! It's hard to say what."
That's what the man said. So I tried to take care
Just to feed Gus a pinch. But it never seemed fair.
'Cause he always looked sad when he gulped down the stuff
And his eyes seemed to tell me, "This isn't enough!"
Then he'd always blow bubbles, as much as to say,
"Come on! Don't be stingy! I'm hungry today!"

Gus *had* to have food.
    Not a spot. But a lot!
No matter what happened.
    I didn't care what.
So, finally, one day,
    poor old Gus looked *so* thin,
I took the whole box
    and I dumped it *all* in!

But the second I did it,
    I saw I'd done wrong.
That fish food, I guess,
    must be terribly strong.
The second Gus ate it,
    he grew twice as long!
He grew twice as thick
    and he grew twice as wide!
Too big for his fishbowl!
    His tail was outside!

He was bursting the glass! He was big as a trout!
I grabbed for the rose bowl. I yanked the rose out.
My mother's best bowl, but I spilled Gustav in it.
But what was the use? 'Cause the very next minute
Gustav was bigger! As big as a shad!
And he looked through the glass and he looked mighty mad
And he splashed and he thrashed, and he burped and he blew,
As much as to tell me, "I blame this on *you*!
This is *YOUR* fault, 'cause you fed me a lot!
Get me out of here quick! Get me out of this spot!"

To the back of the house—to the kitchen, I ran!
I needed more water! I filled up a pan.
I poured Gustav in it as fast as I could,
But he kept right on growing! It did him no good.
I poured him from pot into pot after pot,
But the faster I poured him, the bigger he got.
Then I ran out of pots, but poor Gustav still grew!
Oh, it's awful what one box of fish food can do!

Water! More water! He'll die in the air!
I raced from the kitchen and up the hall stair.
Upstairs to the bathroom! And oh! What a climb!
'Cause the fish in my arms grew and grew all the time!
Each step, he kept groaning and rolling his eyes.
When I got to the top, he was halibut-size!

He was almost too big for a fellow to lug,
But I got to the bathtub and put in the plug
And I turned on the cold-water faucet full blast.
"Gustav," I panted, "you're safe now, at last!
Gustav," I panted, "this tub ought to do.
It holds my whole family. It ought to hold you!"

But it *didn't* hold Gustav. He kept right on growing.
And soon the whole bathtub was full. Overflowing!
And my parents, I knew, would be very upset
'Cause the water was making the bathroom quite wet.
It was up past my ankles! My knees! Past my waist!
And I saw Father's shaving-brush, toothbrush and paste
Bobbing round in the ocean! But what could I do?
'Cause Gustav, my goldfish, still grew and he grew!
He was big as a dolphin! A porpoise! A seal!
Oh, why did I ever feed Gustav that meal!
Just because I was careless and fed him a lot,
I would drown in this bathroom
        as likely as not!

Then *BANG!* With a crash and a terrible roar
And a splintering smash, we burst right through the door!
And Gustav and I shot out into the halls
And back down the stairs like Ni-ag-ara Falls!

Then the first thing I knew,
    we were down in the cellar
And Gustav, my fish,
    was a gi-gantic feller!
Too wild and too dangerous
    to handle alone!
I needed some help!
    So I rushed to the phone
And quick dialed the number
    of Mr. VanBuss,
The man who sold
    Gustav the Goldfish to us:

"Come over, please, mister!
    He's big as a whale!
He's banging the furnace
    to bits with his tail!"

"I knew," sighed the man, "this would happen one day!"
And he hung up the phone and he came right away
With a lot of strange bottles tucked into his vest
And a thing on his back like a medicine chest.
And he took it down cellar and worked underwater
On Gustav for more than an hour and a quarter!

What he did, I don't know. But he must have been wise
'Cause he shrank Gustav back to his regular size!

And he said as he handed my fish back to me,
"It was mighty hard work, boy, but *this* time it's free.
If it happens again, I shall charge a big fee.
So next time, take care!" And he stalked through the door.
Since *then* I've fed Gustav so much and no more.
Since *then* I have *not* fed him more than a *spot*
'Cause something might happen. *And now I know what!*

Tadd and Todd

One twin was named Tadd
And one twin was named Todd.
And they were alike
As two peas in a pod.

They were so much alike, from their hair to their feet,
That people would stare when they walked down the street,
And no one, not even their own mother, knew
Which one was what one, and what one was who.

Now Todd (on the right) was the happier one.
He thought being twins was a whole lot of fun.
He liked it 'cause no one
     could tell him from Tadd.
But Tadd (on the left) . . .
     well, it made him quite sad,
So Tadd (on the left side) one day said to Todd,
"I *don't* want to be like two peas in a pod!"

"I'm going to look different,
     I tell you!" he said.
And Tadd got some ink
     and he dyed his hair red.
"*Now* people will know
     when they see me and you
Which one is what one,
     and what one is who."

"No, no!" answered Todd (on the right).

"If you please,
I like the idea of the pod and two peas."
And Todd grabbed the bottle and quick as a wink
He dyed his own hair with the very same ink!
"Ooooh!" sighed poor Tadd (on the left). "This is bad.
I *still* look like Todd and he *still* looks like Tadd!"
And he worried all day and he fretted all night,
"How *CAN* I look different from Todd (on the right)?"

"It's going to take brains and it's going to take tricks,"
Thought Tadd, and next morning he got up at six.
"I've got to wear clothes of a very strange kind."
So he made a false tail,

which he hitched on behind.
He left off one shoe,

stuck a rose on his toe.
"*NOW* when they see me," said Tadd,

"they will *know*
Which one is what one, and who, without fail.
For *I'll* be the one with the rose and the tail!
But to make *double* sure,

I'll do one more small thing.
I'll catch a queer bird,

which I'll keep on a string.
I'll take the bird with me wherever I go
And the bird and my tail and the rose on my toe
Will show that I'm Tadd, and that Todd is not me,
That I am just I, and that I am not he!"

Thought Tadd, "It's not bad. It's not bad for a start,
But I've got to make *certain* they'll tell us apart.
I'd better, perhaps, get a couple things more."
So he took all his savings and went to a store
And bought a big statue of General Lee Miller,
Who once was a famous old buffalo killer.
That for his shoulder; and then for his back
He strapped on a dog in a brown burlap sack.
"They're heavy," thought Tadd. "And the bag sort of itches.
But people will know, now, which one of us which is!"

"It's mighty good stuff.
But is it enough . . . ?

It *may* be enough, but I can't take a chance.
The whole town must know I am Tadd at first glance."
So Tadd made some stilts more than seven feet high

And he bought an umbrella that came from Shanghai.
Then he spent his last cent for a fat Turkish hat
And seven balloons. Then he said, "That is that.
And *NOW* I'll run home and I'll show brother Todd
We're *NOT* like two peas in a silly old pod!"

But when he got home . . . what a terrible sight!
Tadd (on the left) stared at Todd (on the right)
And saw that his brother was dressed up quite neatly
Exactly like *he* was! *Precisely! COMPLETELY!*
        "You see, Tadd," said Todd,
                "it's high time that you knew
        That *you* look like *me,*
                and that *I* look like *you*
        And you'll *never* look different,
                whatever you do!"
        Then Tadd sort of smiled.
                "Yes, I guess that is true."

And they say that today, when you see Tadd with Todd,
They're *both* having fun being peas in a pod.
And *still* no one knows when they meet with these two
If this one is that one, or that one is this one,
Or which one is what one, or what one is who!

Steak for Supper

When I'm all by myself and there isn't a crowd,
I guess that I sometimes get thinking-out-loud.
And I guess I *was* talking while steering my feet
On the way home for supper down Mulberry Street.
And I must have been thinking 'bout what I would eat,
'Cause I shouted out loud and with all of my might
That we always have steak every Saturday night!

My father had warned me, "Don't babble. Don't bray.
For you never can tell who might hear what you say."
My father had warned me, "Boy, button your lip."
And I guess that I should have. I made a bad slip.
'Cause the minute I said we had steak for our meal,
I noticed an *IKKA* behind at my heel!
And that Ikka was trailing me home for a bite
Of the steak that we have every Saturday night!

I got sort of worried. Our steaks are quite small
And we had none to spare for that Ikka at all.
Then I *really* got worried. The next thing I knew
The Ikka was talking and babbling, too!
That Ikka was waving his wing at a *GRITCH*!
"Come on!" he was calling. "They're terribly rich.
They've *plenty* of steak. And they'll cook it just right
'Cause they always have steak every Saturday night!"

Then the Gritch started giving the come-along sign,
Inviting a *GRICKLE* to get in the line!
"Join up!" called the Gritch. "For I'm sure they'll be able
To set one more place at their dining-room table."
An Ikka, a Gritch and a Grickle to feed!
My mother, I knew, would be angry indeed
And I groaned and I knew that I hadn't been bright
When I bragged we had steak every Saturday night!

And then, *then* the Grickle called out to a NUPPER,
"They always have steak for their Saturday supper!"
"Good gracious!" I gasped. "How the news gets around!
And steak so expensive! A dollar a pound!"
A Nupper for supper! A Gritch! And a Grickle!
And also an Ikka! Oh, boy! What a pickle!

I shivered. I wondered what Father would do
When I walked in the house with that terrible crew.
When Father saw *them,* there's a very good chance
That I'd likely get whaled on the seat of my pants.
And I guess if I did, it would serve me quite right
'Cause I blabbed we had steak every Saturday night.

And the very next second, I groaned, "Oh, good grief!"
When the Nupper called out to a pair of *WILD WHEEF*,
"Come on, you Wild Wheef! What a party we'll make!
For Saturday's supper they always have steak!"
What a mess! Two Wild Wheef! And a Nupper! An Ikka!
A Gritch! And a Grickle! I'd never felt sicker.

I knew that the minute I walked through that door
My mother would faint and my father would roar!
And tomorrow they'd send me to one of those schools
Where they try to train boys how-to-not-act-like-fools!
I reached for the doorknob and trembled with fright
All because I'd said, "Steak every Saturday night!"

I opened the door. Then I stopped with a sniff.
I smelled what was cooking. I took a big whiff.
The Ikka stopped, also, and sniffed at that smell.
And so did the Wheef and the Nupper as well.

The Gritch and the Grickle, they stopped and sniffed, too.
And the moment we sniffed it, we all of us knew
That the stuff that we sniffed *wasn't* steak! *It was stew!*
The butcher who sent it had made a mistake.
For Saturday's supper we didn't have steak!

"Just *stew* . . . ?" gulped the Grickle. *"Just stew! Pooh,* I say!
If they only have *stew,* I don't think I will stay."
"STEW!" they all snorted out loud in disgust,
And they all disappeared in a big cloud of dust!

What luck! I stood safe, all alone in the hall.
My mother and dad hadn't seen them at all!
And from that night to this I have never made slips.
I don't talk when I walk, 'cause I've buttoned my lips.

The Strange Shirt Spot

My mother had warned me:
"Stay out of the dirt."
But there, there I was
With a spot on my shirt!

My brand-new white shirt! And that spot was so sticky,
It wouldn't shake off. It was gummy and gicky.
A terrible spot. This was real gooey goo.
And, brother, I knew what my mother would do
When Mother came home and she saw all that dirt . . . !
I had to get rid of that spot on my shirt!

I hurried upstairs, and from over the tub
I grabbed a big towel and I started to rub.
I rubbed at that spot and I rubbed it real keen.
I rubbed it till, finally, I rubbed the shirt clean.
But then . . . *then* I looked, and I let out a howl.
That spot from the shirt! It was now on the towel!
Now I had to get rid of the big spot of dirt
That had moved to the towel when it moved from my shirt!

I filled up the bathtub. I let it run hot.
I took lots of soap and I scrubbed at that spot
From quarter past three until quarter to four
Till, finally, the spot wasn't there anymore.
Now the towel was all right. It was perfectly white.
My troubles were over. But . . . oh-oh! Not quite!
For the spot that had moved from my shirt to the towel
Was now on the tub! I was sore as an owl!

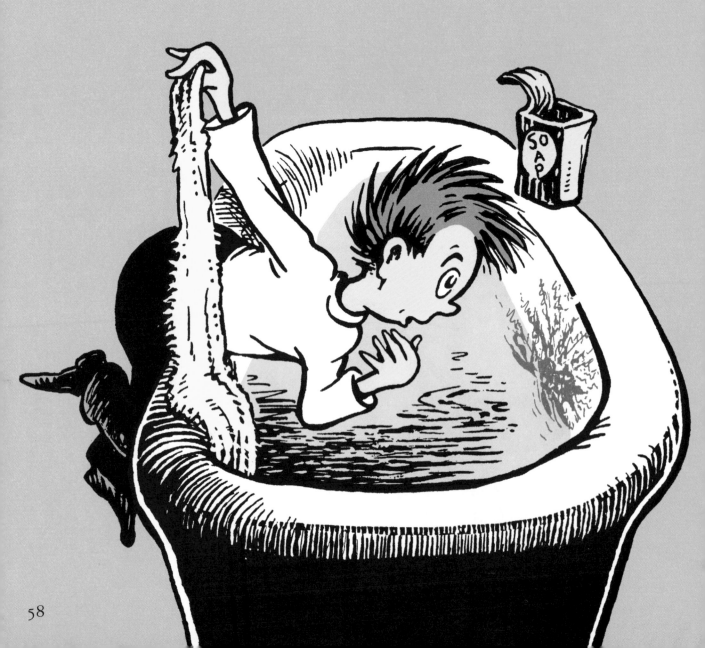

What kind of a spot *was* this spot I had found?
The way the darned thing kept on jumping around!
Now the *tub* needed cleaning! I ran from the room.
I ran to the kitchen. I brought back the broom.
And I swept at that spot till I'd swept it away.
But everything seemed to be crazy today!
For that spot from the tub, from the towel, from the shirt
Was now on the broom! This was mighty queer dirt!

Had to clean up that broom before Mother would find me.
I grabbed a big cloth that was hanging behind me.
I went at that broom with a wipe and a swipe.
Then I saw what had happened. I let out a *"Yipe!"*
For that strange and peculiar, mysterious dirt
From the broom, and the tub, and the towel, and the shirt
Was now on the cloth! This was really a mess!
For the cloth that I'd used was my mother's best dress!

This spot! It was driving me out of my mind!
What a spot—what a spot for a fellow to find!
My troubles were growing. The way it kept going!
Where would it go next? There was no way of knowing.
Oh, how could I stop it? Now what could I do?
Then in walked the cat. And the next thing I knew
The cat bumped the dress. And I almost fell flat.
For the spot from the dress, it was now on the cat!

Then the cat started running all over the place,
With me running after. And, boy! What a chase!
I chased him downstairs. Tumbled down the whole flight.
But, finally, I nabbed him. I grabbed him real tight.
Then I got an idea! I knew just what to do.
I'd put him outside! I'd get rid of the goo!
I laughed. And I put the cat out through the door.
That spot couldn't bother me, now, anymore.

But OOW! Then I looked and I saw that the dirt
Had rubbed off the cat. It was back on my shirt!
Right back where it started! I just couldn't win.
And then, at that moment, my mother walked in.
And, oh! The fast talking that *I* had to do!
I told her the terrible things I'd been through
With the towel, and the tub, and the broom, and the dress,
And the cat, and the shirt, and she said, "Well, I guess
You're lucky you didn't get terribly hurt.
But please, in the future, STAY OUT OF THE DIRT!"

The Great Henry McBride

"It's hard to decide,"
Said young Henry McBride.
"It's terribly, terribly hard to decide.
When a fellow grows up and turns into a man,
A fellow should pick the best job that he can.
But there's *so* many jobs that would be so much fun,
It's terribly hard to decide on just one.

"I *might* be a farmer . . . That sounds pretty good.
That *could* be my job and, now, maybe it should.
I'll buy a big farm somewhere out in the West
And raise giant rabbits. The world's very best!
Yeah! That's what I'll do. That's the way I'll decide.
I'll be the big Rabbit-Man, Henry McBride!

"But now I don't know . . . I'm too smart and too clever
To tie myself down
        just to *one* job forever.
If I could have *two* jobs,
        now that would be swell!
Besides taking care
        of the rabbits I sell,
Why, I could be, also,
        a Doctor as well!
Then people will say
        when they feel sick inside,
'I'll go to the Rabbit-Man, Dr. McBride!'

"The man who does *two* things! Yep! That'll be me,
Doctor and Rabbit-Man, Henry McB.
But why only *two* things . . . ? Say! I could do *three*!
I'll build a big Radio Broadcasting Tower
And broadcast the news
        and the sports every hour!
And then I'll be famous
        and known far and wide
As Broadcaster-Rabbit-Man-
        Doctor McBride!

"Pooh! *Three* jobs is nothing. I still could do more.
I've got lots of brains. It's a cinch. I'll do *four*!
I'll buy myself one of those seal-trainer suits
And train seals to balance big balls on their snoots.
Then people will say, 'Young McBride is sure slick!
He raises fine rabbits while healing the sick,
While broadcasting news and, besides, he's so quick
He's all the time teaching some seal a new trick!'

"And cow-punching's great! So I'll do that! Of course!
I'll do all five jobs on the back of a horse!
And when people see me come galloping by,
They'll cheer and they'll shout, 'What a wonderful guy!
The man who does *everything*! Wow! He's a whiz!
Why, he's got the very best job that there is!
The Seal-Training Doctor! Just look at him ride!
The Broadcasting-Rabbit-Man, Two-Gun McBride!'

"Yep! I'll pick the very best job that I can
When I finally grow up and turn into a man.
But now . . . well, right now when I'm still sort of small,
The *best* job is dreaming, with no work at all."